✦ THE CREATIVE ✦
GAME MASTER'S
TRIVIA & ACTIVITY
✦ BOOK ✦

THE CREATIVE GAME MASTER'S TRIVIA & ACTIVITY BOOK.

Copyright © 2025 by Bluestone Books. All rights reserved.

Any unauthorized duplication in whole or in part or dissemination of this edition by any means (including but not limited to photocopying, electronic devices, digital versions, and the internet) will be prosecuted to the fullest extent of the law.

Bluestone Books
www.bluestonebooks.co

ISBN: 978-1-965636-05-3 (trade paperback)

Printed in the United States of America
10 9 8 7 6 5 4 3 2 1

Puzzles by: Anna Mirabella
Composition by: Twozdai Hulse
Images used under license by Shutterstock.com

IMPORTANT NOTE TO READERS: This book has been written and published for entertainment purposes only. This book is independently authored and published and no sponsorship or endorsement of this book by, and no affiliation with popular tabletop role-playing games or any trademarked brands or products mentioned within is claimed or suggested. All trademarks that appear in this book belong to their respective owners and are used here for informational purposes only.

THE CREATIVE GAME MASTER'S TRIVIA & ACTIVITY BOOK

Test Your Knowledge and Uncover Mind-Blowing Facts about Your Favorite RPG

ANNA MIRABELLA

BLUESTONE BOOKS

Get ready to dust off your game manual to answer these classic D&D trivia questions.

1. What kind of die do you use when playing DUNGEONS & DRAGONS?
   _____

2. **TRUE OR FALSE:** In DUNGEONS & DRAGONS, you have to choose a pre-made character provided by the DM.
   _____

3. What are the six ability scores that each player has?
   _____

4. What is the effect of a candle?
   _____

5. Navigator's tools are used for what purpose?
   _____

6. What attribute is recommended to be the highest for wizards?
   _____

7. Where can celestials be found?
   _____

8. Monster statistics can also be known as
   _____

9. A net has no effect on which types of creatures?
   _____

FUN FACT

DUNGEONS & DRAGONS was created and published in 1974 by two American game designers. Earnest Gary Gygax and David Arneson. The first rule book consisted of fifty pages. Iterations since have nearly tripled in size!

More and More Monsters

In the DUNGEONS & DRAGONS 5th Edition manual, there are fourteen categories that monsters are placed into. Use the clues to identify all fourteen monster types and write them in the puzzle.

ACROSS
1. Wicked creatures that live on the Lower Planes
3. Necromancy is used to bring these beings to life
6. Unnatural, terrifying creatures
8. Giant reptile-like creatures of ancient origin
10. Good beings native to the Upper Planes
11. Common creatures with an established culture and language
12. Humanoid in shape, but larger in size
13. Creatures like the shambling mound and the treant

FUN FACT
Back in 1986, there were only six categories introduced in the *Creature Catalogue* supplement.

DOWN
1. Creatures that include pixies, dryads, and satyrs
2. Monsters from the elemental plains
4. Alien beings
5. Creatures that are created rather than born
7. Gelatinous, shapeless monsters
9. Nonhumanoid creatures including dinosaurs and animals

Scrambled Spells for Clerics

Clerics are just one type of magic wielders in DUNGEONS & DRAGONS. These divine souls act as emissaries between the planes of the gods and the mortal world. Acting as both strong warriors and devout healers, clerics champion the deities they serve with powerful spells. Use the hints below each item to unscramble the names of some cleric spells.

1. **Dehat adWr** _____
   Hint: Touch a creature or person to grant them some protection against dying.

2. **uendaGci** _____
   Hint: Using this spell, the player gets to roll an extra d4 to add to an ability.

3. **Bsels** _____
   Hint: You can use this spell on up to 3 other people.

4. **Fmlae Sketir** _____
   Hint: Divine fire from the heavens is cast in a specific location of your choosing.

5. **qthauEeark** _____
   Hint: Cast a tremor on the ground that shakes in a 100-foot radius.

6. **itviaDnion** _____
   Hint: You can ask a single question with this spell.

7. **loyH ruAa** _____
   Hint: Creatures of your choice in a 30-foot radius can emit a dim light from a divine light you cast.

8. **uerT gSieen** _____
   Hint: This spell gives a creature the ability to see locked doors and other things.

9. **sAatlr Poroncjite** _____
   Hint: This 9th level spell takes an hour to cast.

10. **iyRievfv** _____
    Hint: Return a creature to life.

11. **siRea eaDd** _____
    Hint: This is a 5th level necromancy spell.

12. **elBda rraeirB** _____
    Hint: Summon a wall of blades using magical energy.

13. **sHoere saFte** _____
    Hint: Eat food and drink for an hour for some beneficial effects.

14. **Cmeunom** _____
    Hint: You can ask your deity up to three questions.

15. **aHel** _____
    Hint: Cure a teammate of your choosing.

Satchel-Filling Seek and Find

Every adventurer needs a satchel (or *an entire camp*) full of items to aid them in their journey. Find all of the common pieces of equipment an adventurer might pack to complete their quest in the wordfind below.

```
N E H R Y D R E D D A L B T
H I N E O K M N G B V P L T
O K X O L P Z D A V M M T J
U C T O T M E R E A P O L E
R A S Y T S D S L E R R A B
G P E G B I T B E D R O L L
L K H M N M T E R R A Q J L
A C C G E E L N H B L T Z Z
S A T N F D H C A W O G B Y
S B T I D O U C R R G Z M R
Z S N I R O U N C Y R J M P
M K F N P S P H M Q L J Z N
```

Abacus	Bedroll	Hourglass	Pole
Antitoxin	Chest	Knife	Rope
Backpack	Fiddle	Ladder	Torch
Barding	Helm	Lamp	Vestments
Barrel	Horn	Pouch	Whetstone

A D & D Blessing

Decode the message to discover a popular D&D blessing. Each letter in the phrase has been replaced with a random letter or number. Some of the letters have been filled in for you.

A	B	C	D	E	F	G	H	I	J	K	L	M	N	O	P	Q	R	S	T	U	V	W	X	Y	Z
19				6				16																	

___ A ___ ___ ___ E ___ I ___ E
1 19 10   7 11 6   24 16 8 6

___ E ___ E ___ E ___ ___ I ___
26 6   6 17 6 12   16 25

___ ___ ___ ___ ___ A ___ ___ ___
10 14 5 12   21 19 17 14 12

Journey By Mount

Even in the multiverse, adventurers need a way to travel. While there may not be cars and trains like we have in our modern world, boats and animals are viable options depending on where your adventurer finds themselves. But be sure you have proficiency in riding before trying to tame an animal to mount! Travel through this puzzle and try to find all of the vehicles and mounts listed.

```
X I B D T G B F V O Z V Y S F L T B
R G L S V T V X D O F L G M G C N E
J B E L E P H A N T M O J S E Y D U
X O A I N T B R E V D N P O X L D S
E O E I S B N H P O V G U O W T G H
Y Y Z I R X S S F I M S N Q N G T L
F P L G C S Q V B M U H T U W Y G V
H W A A M Y H K T A L I K N A L K V
R A L L H Q W I N S E P P F R Z W D
V D I L S D Q E P T O P W H H C A Q
I H W E A M V W M I O J Y F O E R Y
T O K Y T M H K J F Y W P D R K S C
V R R O W B O A T F B M Q L S D H A
G S H N M H A B H Z F N U R E R I M
U E P J V K P P K E E L B O A T P E
D R G U F S I E U A K U S C H U B L
C S P A O Z L Y V Y G H N P D G N R
H O L N L J Y I G V D B E Z L X K B
```

airship	keelboat	rowboat
camel	longship	warhorse
elephant	mastiff	warship
galley	mule	
horse	pony	

FUN FACT

Larger ships require a group of hirelings to help navigate and maintain them.

Spells Fit for a Warlock Crossword

Warlocks are just one of many character classes that players can choose when creating their adventurer. These magic-wielding heroes get their powers from making pacts with mysterious supernatural beings. Their goal is to find knowledge hidden in the multiverse. To do this, warlocks access a multitude of powerful spells that they can cast at any level! Can you name these mystifying spells that warlocks are able to use?

FUN FACT

At Level 2, warlocks begin to gain access to special invocations, some of which players can even use against their own team!

ACROSS

2 Players whisper magical words that cause a creature to become hostile
3 Players spread magical darkness for a 15-foot radius
4 Players grant a creature they touch with the ability to understand any language it hears
6 Players attempt to send a visible creature to another place of existence
7 Players curse a visible creature
8 Players cast a phantasmal image of the target's worst fears
9 Players can make a painfully loud ringing noise erupt near a chosen spot
10 Players cast this necromancy spell to drain moisture and vitality from a target

DOWN

1 Players can make a creature they touch turn invisible
5 By whispering distracting words, players cause their target to make a Wisdom saving throw
8 After the player touches a willing creature, it gains a flying speed of 60 feet

Elf Names Word Search

Up until their 100th birthday, elves are considered children and are referred to as such. When they finally mature, they take on adult names that they choose themselves. These names are uniquely important to each elven individual and rarely reflect specific gender norms. Below are some common adult names for elves. Can you find them all?

```
O W I F G F O L T X O H A K C Y E H
D R O L E N Z A T C B B T D M V U L
W W M G D H G U O F I E E Z T Q D R
W C K K Z D H C T I R B D R H T X E
Z R G J T D O I C T E D E N R B R D
R X N I H Z P A L W L E T U W I J O
N U X F A N R N U N H D D K H D A M
Y H P K R V L G A L I N N D A N C N
Q I S L I E B F E L O S I A L U H T
L S H G V A L A N T H E A P S R L Q
K Z A D O L A Z A T H P N B Z P T
E B N R L U O H S D H V S E O V N X
A U A M I K S L A H R B A R R C B W
D Z I G C E V X F D C I Z D I E P C
R D R U S I L I A J A Z E Y A N N
A N R A N T I N U A M R N D B N H Q
N L A T P E X C U A E L A R I R I L
E Y O B Y Q F A N B T O V I G D Z A
```

adran	drusilia	rolen
adrie	felosial	sariel
aelar	galinndan	shanairra
atinua	hadarai	tharivol
berrian	laucian	vadania
birel	peren	valanthe

FUN FACT

Even though elves choose an adult name, it isn't uncommon for people who knew them when they were younger to continue using their child name.

Beyond the Table and into the Pages

Dungeons & Dragons literature comes in many forms. Whether it be a core rulebook, a campaign adventure, or a graphic novel ... there are tons of books to satiate your D&D hunger. So, put down the dice and take out your reading glasses. It's time to see how much you know about D&D books and unscramble these words!

1. **Parleys anoHobkd**

   _____

   Hint: The official rulebook with comprehensive knowledge on how to play the game.

2. **enorsMt lMuana**

   _____

   Hint: A core rulebook about the different creatures you may come across in your campaign.

3. **unnDoeg staresM Gueid**

   _____

   Hint: A guide showing how to run a Dungeons & Dragons campaign.

4. **vEe fo Runi**

   _____

   Hint: A high-level adventure for fans of Vecna.

5. **hTe Dusrdi aCll**

   _____

   Hint: A prequel to *Honor Among Thieves* that features a druid named Doric.

6. **Horno nAgmo hieTsev**

   _____

   Hint: A retelling of the events in the popular 2023 movie.

7. **idkMarrnebe**

   _____

   Hint: A graphic novel about popular villains from the D&D franchise.

8. **arrWoisr nAd spenoaW**

   _____

   Hint: An illustrated guide that explains the different types of fighters you can be and what they need to fight.

9. **mTbo of nioAilnthian**

   _____

   Hint: An adventure surrounding the necromantic artifact, the Soulmonger.

10. **Crues fo Srdtha**

    _____

    Hint: An adventure for players level 1-10 about uncovering Ravenloft's mysteries.

FUN FACT

The 5th Edition of the *Dungeons & Dragons Player's Handbook* was released in early access on September 3, 2024.

True Adventurer Trivia

Get ready to test your RPG fandom knowledge and answer as many trivia questions as you can.

1. How do you score a critical hit?
   _____

2. What does heroic inspiration allow the player to do?
   _____

3. **TRUE OR FALSE:** Players must be proficient with a weapon in order to use it.
   _____

4. For how long can players use a mount to gain double distance?
   _____

5. How long does a combat round last in the game world?
   _____

6. What does initiative represent in combat?
   _____

7. **TRUE OR FALSE:** Players may interact with a single object on their turn without using an action point.
   _____

8. How many human ethnic groups are there in the Forgotten Realms?
   _____

Potions, Elixirs, and Antidotes

Every good adventurer carries with them a satchel full of potions and elixirs. You never know when you'll need to heal yourself or your party, gain access to specific abilities, or even give your team some extra resistance buffs. Using the clues below, can you name all of the potions your adventurer may stumble upon in their journey?

1. otnPio of quuAseo rFom

   _____

   Hint: The person who drinks this turns into a pool of water for ten minutes.

2. liO fo teseeahnrEls

   _____

   Hint: An entity covered in this steps foot into the border regions of the Ethereal Plane for an hour.

3. uMymm tRo eotdiAtn

   _____

   Hint: A pale gray potion with dust swirling inside. It cures a user touched by a mummy.

4. Eirlix fo tlhaeH

   _____

   Hint: This potion restores some HP to the user.

5. noPoti of gyFinl

   _____

   Hint: Characters who drink this gain the ability to fly.

6. hPrtlie fo veLo

   _____

   Hint: A potion used to charm another creature.

7. Oli of pnrhSaess

   _____

   Hint: When applied to slashing or piercing weapon, it gains +3 bonus to attack and damage rolls.

8. inoPot fo ityVtlai

   _____

   Hint: Removes the poisoned and exhausted conditions.

9. Bldoo of het yaoLrtecpnh neoidAtt

   _____

   Hint: Heals the curse of Lycanthropy.

10. tBdolet rehBat

    _____

    Hint: A potion that grants the user the effect of the "Gust of Wind" spell when they exhale.

11. itnPoo of atlWuhcf seRt

    _____

    Hint: Whoever drinks it can stay awake during a long rest.

12. hsxTolnetsai Attidone

    _____

    Hint: A potion that changes its color every time you look at it. It cures the polymorph effect.

FUN FACT

Prior to the new rules in 2024, drinking a potion required the use of an action.

CANTRIPS CROSSWORD

Magic wielding characters can access special spells called cantrips. These cantrips don't take up any action slots and can be used an infinite number of times without wasting any resources. While they're weaker in nature than other spells, these cantrips are not to be taken lightly. Some create powerful openings or allow players to achieve goals outside of battle. Can you identify the names of some popular cantrips?

ACROSS
1. Players can touch an object and repair a single tear or break
6. Players imbue the quarterstaff or club they are holding with nature's power
7. Players imbue a creature they touch with vitality
9. Players cause a cloud of parasites to appear on a selected creature
10. Players form numbing frost on a creature they can see

DOWN
2. After a player touches a willing creature, they can roll a d4 and add the result to an ability check
3. Within range, players can manifest a minor wonder
4. After a player touches a willing creature, they can roll a d4 and add it to a saving throw
5. Players gain an advantage on charisma checks with a chosen creature
8. This makes an item shine bright in a 20-foot radius

FUN FACT
Some of the most popular cantrips that players like to use are Message, Guidance, and Booming Blade.

Cindergem Maze

Make your way to the cindergem at the center of the maze.

START

Out of this World Word Search

Dungeons & Dragons campaigns take place in more than one world. They can sprawl across multiple lands and even planes of existence. The Outer Planes is one such area in the multiverse that exists outside of the Material Plane and in the Astral Plane. It's where you'll find deities, demons, celestials, and devils. You won't need to travel far through the multiverse to find these locations in the puzzle below.

```
V O D H F C C P C D C U W R H C Q J
M K U R M O K P U A B O T J U M E N
N W A T Q Z A T O M R Z K A A C J O
B N A R L W O C Q D E C L O Q R F E
Y M R F C A G B V N D C E I Z R N L
H R B O P A N G E A U T H R M S A Y
U M O J A J D D O A V F T A I B I S
V S R M N H P I S Y S M Z Y N T O I
N Q E E D A A C A B H T W W Y U R U
W O A S E A G D V X X T L V K P S M
Y Y A R M W L E E C H F H A E T R N
B Q B F O A H Y H S X K C O N B B N
Y L Y K N H F O Y E A P U R S D P M
T L S F I G T W Y S N Z B S N J S Y
O X S F U J O O L Q G N U C V W F J
P B Z V M P F T B H K A A Y X O I K
I J Y L C S V T X D X Q R T J K L D
A C H E R O N O D J L X F D W K Y M
```

abyss	beastlands	gehenna	outlands
acheron	bytopia	hades	pandemonium
arborea	carceri	limbo	ysgard
arcadia	elysium	mechanus	

FUN FACT

The entire D&D universe shares cosmology for the Outer Planes.

Ruby Maze

Make your way to the sparkling ruby at the end of the maze.

START

True Adventurer Trivia

Get ready to test your RPG fandom knowledge and answer as many trivia questions as you can about dragonborns.

1. Who are the gods that have blessed the eggs of the dragonborn's ancestors?

2. Do dragonborns have wings and a tail?

3. What color are the scales of a dragonborn usually?

4. Are dragonborns shorter or taller than 5 feet?

5. Does a dragonborn usually weigh more or less than 200 pounds?

6. How many fingers does a dragonborn have?

7. How common are dragonborns in the DUNGEONS & DRAGONS multiverse?

8. What ability score is increased for dragonborns?

9. At what age do dragonborns reach adulthood?

10. What is a dragonborn's speed?

11. What is a dragonborn's size class?

12. How many draconic ancestries can you choose from when making your dragonborn?

Shopping Spree Price Match

On their journey, adventurers may run out of supplies or find a need for something they never had on hand. Before entering any dungeon or initiating combat, adventurers should stock up at their local merchants and unload items that are weighing them down. Can you match the items with their actual cost in the game?

Acid	100 GP
Antitoxin	2 GP
Book	1 GP
Fine Clothes	40 GP
Tent	10 GP
Magnifying Glass	25 GP
Backpack	15 GP
Bedroll	2 GP
Basic Poison	50 GP
Scholar's Pack	2 GP
Lock	25 GP
Shovel	100 GP

Action-Packed Adventure Word Search

At the start of each turn, players can use a single action. Actions typically don't include communication or movement. Different classes allow adventurers to take bonus actions. While there are twelve actions listed in the player manual, adventurers and creatures can engage in other activities depending on the situation. Use the search action to find all the actions in the puzzle before your turn ends.

```
D L A S J O M M R R D X S J U A B S
Y X R I O Y F M L W A V W N V T G Y
D I S E N G A G E C S Q I H E L P A
M H V T I V B P Q W H F M K B W H P
X K N N F S Y G G H E U Q H V N P H
V D S B Q T E I I U F S T X K C Y F
Q E A T X J R A I K J T H I V Y I Z
G C Q T U Q S H R J C F S D L Y T V
Q S A N T D N I S C V U A H O I F Z
R B C H R A Y A O F H I D I K D Z B
E S C A P E C C L I M B M D D H G E
A T T P G E O K N B C J G E V L N E
D V U C B E G R A P P L E R K N X D
Y B E W L S H O V E V V X T X N M I
V C M D I N R T R I N F L U E N C E
F A L F K M O V E Y K G X G I C K N
F Y V O B S J C G M A G I C N I Z S
S H D G G W S H Q Z P S U C J K T Z
```

attack	disengage	grapple	influence	ready	study
climb	dodge	help	magic	search	swim
dash	escape	hide	move	shove	utilize

FUN FACT

Players cannot use two actions simultaneously.

WEARABLES

You can't step foot into a dangerous dungeon or a perilous fight without any armor! Different pieces of armor and accessories grant different abilities and bonuses. Be sure to try out different combinations to see what keeps your party alive the longest. All of the items below are magical accessories, cloaks, boots, and other things your character can wear. Use the clues to unscramble them.

1. loeCsth fo ennMgdi

   _____

   Hint: This wearable item can fix itself when damaged with daily use.

2. toBos fo nrtlWanide

   _____

   Hint: When worn, these shoes grant cold resistance.

3. lsadetB Golgegs

   _____

   Hint: This item emits a bright light that grants the user the blinded condition.

4. mutAle of het evtDou

   _____

   Hint: An amulet with a symbol of a deity on it. It gives the wearer a bonus to their spell attack power.

5. Colka of ipeDmctselan

   _____

   Hint: This item creates an illusion of the wearer's location and offers a disadvantage on attack rolls against them.

6. eritcCl of Hunma rcftPioene

   _____

   Hint: This headpiece, when attuned, turns the wearer into an attractive human.

7. lorcokkCw Autmel

   _____

   Hint: The wearer can roll a ten for attack once a day.

8. aeDdr mlHe

   _____

   Hint: When worn, this steel helmet makes the user's eyes glow red.

9. Crnow fo iLes

   _____

   Hint: This wearable artifact grants the ability to use perfect disguise when attuned.

10. ulneGtsat of gOer Porwe

    _____

    Hint: These gloves grant the wearer strength of nineteen.

11. tHa fo issDiueg

    _____

    Hint: Allows the wearer to cast the "Disguise Self" spell.

12. r'sestJe aMsk

    _____

    Hint: When worn, you gain Charismatic Focus, Marvelous Escape, and Topsy-Turvy.

13. rarBsce of eerCilyt

    _____

    Hint: When worn, this item increases the wearers speed by 10 feet.

FUN FACT

A character can only be attuned to three magic items at once.

Player Feats to Beat Crossword

At various points in their adventures, players get to choose feats that enhance their talents and abilities. In the 5th Edition of the official Dungeons & Dragons handbook, there are seventy-five feats to choose from. Ranging from giving players proficiency in new skills to gaining advantages on various rolls, there are bound to be a few feats that will help bolster your character! Test your knowledge of D&D and see if you can name all the feats in the puzzle below!

FUN FACT
Some feats can be chosen more than one time.

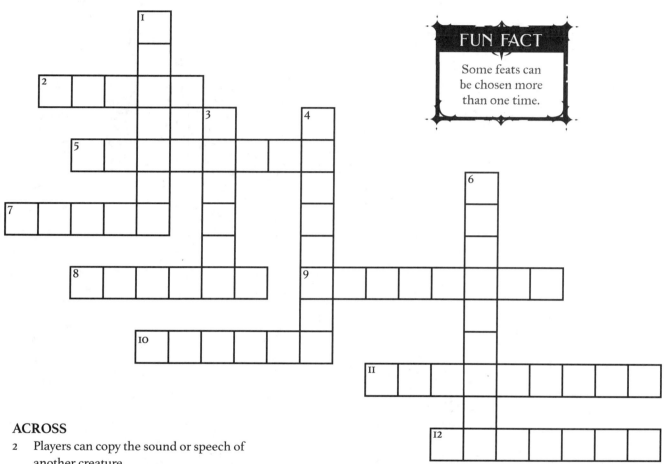

ACROSS
2. Players can copy the sound or speech of another creature
5. Players gain proficiency with the poisoner's kit
7. Players can force a creature to re-roll an attack against them
8. Players can restore hit points to another creature or stabilize them
9. Players can learn three languages
10. Players have proficiency in firearms
11. Allows players to read lips
12. Players can climb and stand up more quickly

DOWN
1. Players gain proficiency with either a skill, tool, or language
3. A player's speed is increased by 10 feet
4. Players have an advantage on attack rolls when trying to grapple
6. Players gain +1 to a single ability and gain proficiency in saving throws with it

Sapphire Maze

Make your way to the sparkling sapphire at the end of the maze.

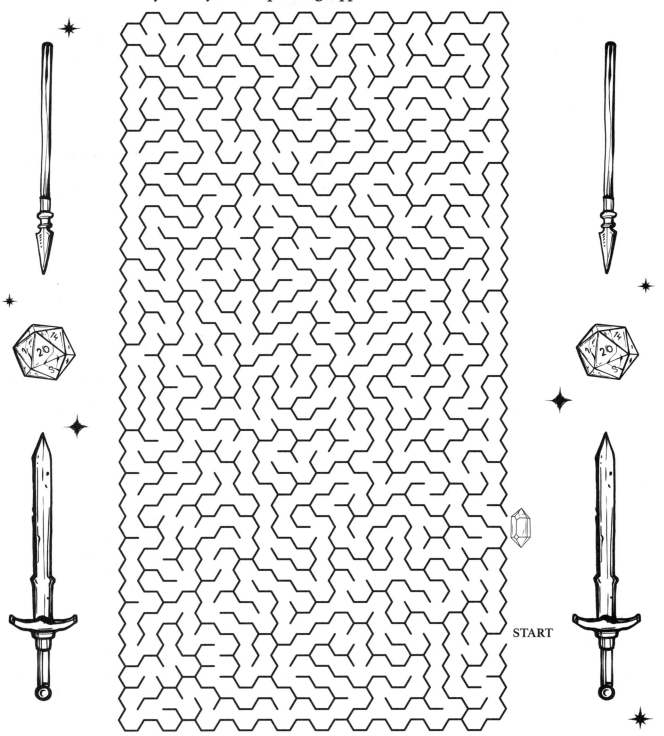

START

Speak Their Languages Crossword

With so many character races and backgrounds, it's no wonder there are a multitude of languages that the people of the multiverse speak. Common language is the most used speech among humanoid creatures. However, most species have their own ways of communicating among each other. While the languages in the puzzle below are rare, you might come across them in your adventures. Can you identify them all?

ACROSS
1. The secret language belonging to the druids
3. The language belonging to aberrations
6. A language using vibrations to create a humming sound
8. The language belonging to devils
9. A form of communication unique to rogues

DOWN
2. The language spoken in the underdark
4. The language belonging to fey creatures
5. A language spoken amongst those in the Upper Planes
7. The language belonging to demons

FUN FACT
Depending on their class and backgrounds, characters can learn up to four languages at Level 1.

True Adventurer Trivia

Get ready to test your RPG fandom knowledge and answer as many trivia questions as you can about dwarves.

1. What ability score increases if you choose to play a dwarf?
   _____

2. What alignment do most dwarves fall into?
   _____

3. What advantage does Dwarven Resilience grant you?
   _____

4. What four weapons do dwarves have proficiency with?
   _____

5. What are the two dwarf subraces?
   _____

6. What ability score increases for hill dwarves?
   _____

7. Which dwarf subrace is granted Dwarven Toughness?
   _____

8. What ability score increases for mountain dwarves?
   _____

9. How long can a dwarf live?
   _____

True Adventurer Trivia

Get ready to test your RPG fandom knowledge and answer as many trivia questions about character backgrounds and classes as you can.

1. How many backgrounds are there in the 5th Edition player manual?

2. What feat does an acolyte gain?

3. What skill proficiencies does an entertainer have?

4. What tool proficiency does a hermit have?

5. What ability scores does a soldier focus on?

6. In the crafter origin, you gain proficiency with how many action tools?

7. In the Musician origin, what does encouraging song do?

8. Which of these feats are repeatable: skilled, healer, chef, or grappler?

9. Which of these is not an origin feat: lucky, savage, attacker, athlete, or magic initiate?

10. How many times can a druid usually use Wild Shape?

11. A character's background gives them proficiency in how many skills?

12. How many ability scores does a player list when creating a new character?

Dwarf Clan Names Word Search

Dwarf clans find themselves prospering underneath the mountains where they can mine gems and ore. Dwarves take these precious metals to forge weapons, accessories, and other items of value. But what they can't find underground or craft themselves, they're able to trade with other nations. The center of these dwarven kingdoms are clans which determine a dwarf's social standing. To be clan-less is the worst fate a dwarf can suffer! Here are some well-known dwarven clans. Can you find all of them?

```
D Z S E B B N J Z Z N D D N V K F L
Q G T P A X U E Y R F D X D R D R E
Y E R B T W J P S I O T H U B P K I
Z R A G T T M Y L O D E R R L Q R F
A B K Z L T H K M N F T P V W Z V
Q F E I E D B A L D E R K W H L P R
A N L C H T T O R U N N D L I P N U
W W N I A H E B F W L U T G E H R M
V E Y R M U C X R I A K Q D W B O N
O P F O M G N S C A R X L C K D L A
C K Y N E U O G N L W E R T N C V H
Y C K F R L D R A Q C N F R M D A E
H S Z I A U D T U R T O A O L R Z I
D J R S F Q C H P N T G F N R I G M
B M Y T Z F C V N I N H Q D V G T X
H O L D E R H E K J W D V F C I E I
A K D F R O S T B E A R D R A C L R
Q Q I U A L R T W E Y C P P B F O S
```

balderk	frostbeard	loderr	torunn
battlehammer	gorunn	lutgehr	ungart
brawnanvil	holderhek	rumnaheim	
fireforge	ironfist	strakeln	

FUN FACT

Even dwarves who don't live within the walls of their kingdoms will invoke their clans and ancient ancestors.

Race You There Crossword

In the 5th Edition of the *Dungeons & Dragons Player's Handbook*, there are ten core races that players can select for their adventurers. However, there are even more species mentioned in the supplementary manuals! Each species has its own unique cultural history as well as defining traits and stats.

ACROSS

3. The god Corellon created this species
6. The ancestors of this species hatched from the eggs of metallic dragons
7. A species that descended from giants
9. A species of diverse creature found throughout the multiverse

FUN FACT

Prior to 2024, character races determined stat bonuses, but in the newest edition of the manual, these have been moved to character backgrounds.

DOWN

1. A species born in the Lower Planes
2. A species with a spark of the Upper Planes despite being mortals
4. A species created by the gods of invention and illusions
5. A species created by a deity of the forge
8. A species created by the god Gruumsh

PEARL MAZE

Make your way to the shining pearl at the end of the maze.

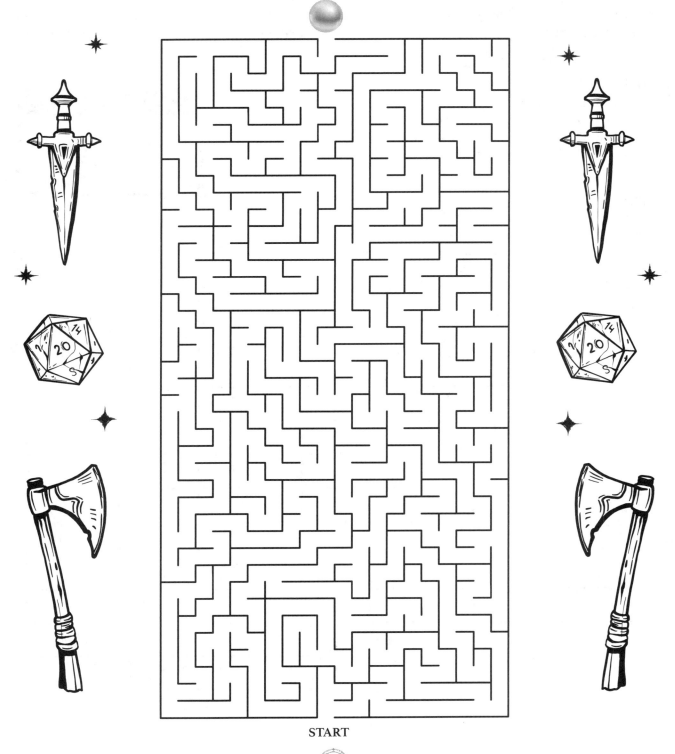

START

Schools of Magic Crossword

In Dungeons & Dragons, spells are sorted into eight categories. These are often referred to as schools of magic. The goal of these groups is to help describe each spell and what they can be used for. Many players use this system to help build their character. Class is in session. Only the players most proficient in magic will be able to name all eight schools and place them in the right order.

ACROSS
4. Focuses on dealing damage
6. Focuses on defensive spells meant to protect and strengthen the user
7. Focuses on enhancing the user's team with buffs
8. Focuses on altering and manipulating the minds of others

DOWN
1. Focuses on gathering information
2. Focuses on manipulating dead targets
3. Focuses on creating objects and summoning creatures
5. Focuses on tricking players by having them see or sense things that are not there

FUN FACT
The schools of magic don't have rules of their own, but they are often referred to in other rules.

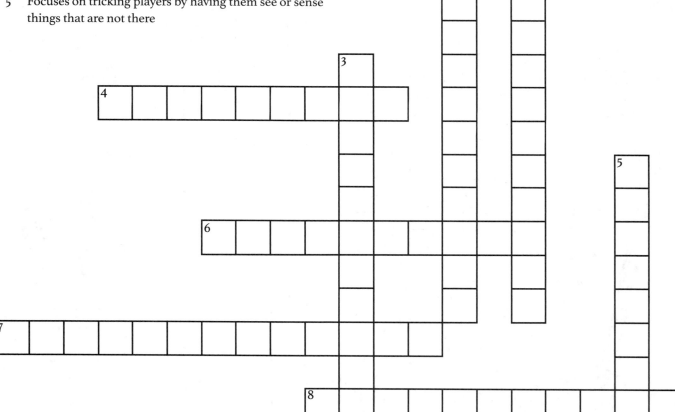

Popular Campaigns

Campaigns are the backbone of any Dungeons & Dragons experience. A campaign is the adventure that players embark on after creating their characters. While there are several officially licensed adventure modules, many experienced DMs have chosen to create their own. Unscramble the letters below using the clues to find the names of these popular D&D campaigns.

1. hTe iRse of amaTti

   _____

   Hint: Players fight against the five headed draconic goddess in this campaign.

2. sLot nMei fo hPenerldva

   _____

   Hint: A campaign meant for first level players that has players fighting the Black Spider to reclaim a mine and restore peace to the area.

3. utO of het syAsb

   _____

   Hint: In this campaign, players are captured by drow in the Underdark and must find a way to stop unleashed demons from destroying the world.

4. klapndCeee yseMiestr

   _____

   Hint: This anthology contains many different one-shot adventure modules.

5. Gstohs fo thlsSaamr

   _____

   Hint: This popular adventure module is nautical themed and takes place in and near the water.

6. Tbmo of ilnnAhtaoiin

   _____

   Hint: In this module, released in 2017, players try to stop a plot to steal the world's souls.

7. rteWdeeap Danrog iHset

   _____

   Hint: Players go on a treasure hunt by exploring clues left by the adventurer Volothamp Geddarm.

8. tSorm iKngs nThreud

   _____

   Hint: When giants start to take over the Sword Coast, players must band together and find out why.

9. Haodr of teh gnrDoa ueneQ

   _____

   Hint: Players must stop the Cult of the Dragon, Red Wizards of Thay, and their dragon allies who are trying to free Tiamat.

FUN FACT

The majority of D&D campaigns take place in the Forgotten Realms.

42

True Adventurer Trivia

Get ready to test your RPG fandom knowledge and answer as many trivia questions as you can about television and movies based on the game.

1. In which popular Netflix show does the main cast name the monsters they face after classic D&D monsters?
   _____

2. In 1982, which movie was released featuring Tom Hanks that depicts a college student obsessed with a D&D-style game?
   _____

3. In which famous Steven Spielberg movie are the main character and his older brother seen playing DUNGEONS & DRAGONS?
   _____

4. How many officially licensed D&D movies are there?
   _____

5. What is the title of the third official DUNGEONS & DRAGONS movie?
   _____

6. The newest DUNGEONS & DRAGONS movie, *Honor Among Thieves*, made about how much money in the box office worldwide?
   A) 150 million
   B) 208 million
   C) 250 million

7. What year did the first official D&D movie release?
   A) 1985
   B) 1995
   C) 2000

8. What year did the animated D&D series come out?
   A) 1983
   B) 1987
   C) 1993

> **FUN FACT**
> When dealing with certain races like humans, gnomes will give only three names out: their personal name, a clan name, and a nickname. They usually choose whichever is most fun to speak out loud.

9. How many seasons of the animated DUNGEONS & DRAGONS television series were there?
   _____

Gnome Nicknames Word Search

Gnomes love the idea of names and find pleasure in giving each other different ones. Gnomes can get names from their clan elders, uncles, aunts, and parents. As such, many gnomes will have over a dozen names just for themself! Here are just a few examples of nicknames a gnome may choose for themselves or others in their clan. See if you can find them all!

```
O N E S H O E D N I F N I P P E R H
I A S H H E A R T H U S V H H H T H
N L M M Y Y T C S T T M S G Q R G O
B H X G V D O U B L E L O C K E F J
V I G R A Z P O B Q G O K X P O C K
H Z R S L H C T V W T H H O Q D L B
Z D F P E S T R U M B L E D U C K Z
G T Q L S T S R J F K C S L F S H X
G W E W L R Q L S I T E R Q F P U B
E A Y B O H Z Y P L T F M X N A Z A
P B N J S C T F O C M F Z S J R F D
L J T A H Q V Q R H F W I S O K L G
D M W K P A K C U B G C T P L L Q E
E X V N A N C Q O A O L W D Q E J R
S H W L S E C F H T X O T S R G S B
M J P G N I M X P T Y A F C K E K T
Z M A Y K T N L I E T K P S G M C N
K E E Z V M U V I R N H V D Z M F Y
```

aleslosh	cloak	fnipper	pock
ashhearth	doublelock	nim	sparklegem
badger	filchbatter	oneshoe	strumbleduck

Elemental Crystal Maze

Make your way to the elemental crystal at the end of the maze.

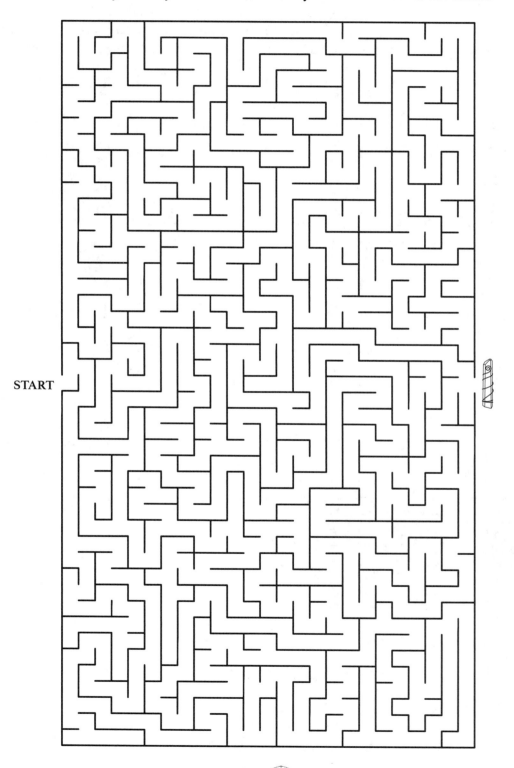

True Adventurer Trivia

Get ready to test your RPG fandom knowledge and answer as many trivia questions as you can about elves.

1. How many pounds do elves usually weigh?

   _____

2. How tall are elves usually?

   _____

3. Do elves prefer to live in smaller forest villages or larger cities?

   _____

4. The first elves were created by which god?

   _____

5. What is the lifespan of an elf?

   _____

6. What are the three subraces of elves?

   _____

7. If you are an elf, what ability score increases?

   _____

8. What alignment do drow fall under?

   _____

9. What is the elf's walking speed?

   _____

10. What do elves have proficiency in?

    _____

11. Which elven subrace can learn an extra language?

    _____

EMERALD MAZE

Make your way to the sparkling emerald at the center of the maze.

START

49

Character Backgrounds Word Search

After choosing your character's class and race, you'll need to take a look at their background. A character's background encompasses the kind of job or lifestyle they had prior to their adventure. Not only does your character's background help shape their personality, but it also provides additional stat boosts. Some common backgrounds are hidden in the word search below. Can you find them all?

```
Q Y R L H G M E R C H A N T J Q D P
J H P T N X P F Z U K A Y N O B L E
C A C O L Y T E X T E K A G H H T H
F H Z C C Y D D F F A R M E R A T U
Z Q A Q Z R G K S W Y R U K M M S Z
F E T R B W I B E Q A T U B M H J E
L Q S C L L N M Z R P Y E F P J S X
R G M O T A W A I O V P F Z R U A W
F J Q O B L T E V N N P O A Z U V D
B Z A R T I S A N M A Q L R R Y H Q
H S S C Z F M X N G O L S U F E E M
S L L C V Q L L P S U B Q A E A R Y
E N T E R T A I N E R A U D G J M U
U W F G H I W I J Y Y V R X B E I R
R R Z Z U U B R D W M T X D J R T Q
V C O Y O Q G E J G G U I D E N Q B
B T Y U D Y B S A I L O R Q J P F K
W F S O L D I E R T V Z M K G X D G
```

acolyte
artisan
charlatan
criminal
entertainer
farmer
guard
guide
hermit
merchant
noble
sage
sailor
scribe
soldier
wayfarer

FUN FACT

A character's background includes five parts: their ability scores, feat, skill proficiencies, tool proficiency, and equipment.

Human Ethnicities Crossword

Humans are the youngest race to show up in the multiverse. With shorter lifespans than other races, they have not had any less impact on the world around them. In fact, humans are able to outlive their shorter lifespans with vast legacies that exist even after they've died. As the most common race in Faerûn, it is no surprise that there are many human ethnicities that have spread throughout the multiverse! Using the clues, can you identify all the human ethnicities mentioned in the player manual?

ACROSS
6. These humans, with yellowish-bronze skin and black hair, are the most powerful ethnic group in Kara-Tur
7. These humans hail from the Northwest of Faerun and have tawny to fair skin
8. These humans are shorter than average humans and have brown skin, eyes, and hair
9. These tall and slim humans are from the eastern and southeastern shores of the Inner Sea

DOWN
1. These humans usually have green or brown eyes and come from the central lands of Faerun
2. These tall humans are fair-skinned and have blue or gray eyes
3. These humans live on the Sword Coast and have a medium build and height
4. These humans have dark mahogany skin and live on the southern shore of the Inner Sea
5. These humans, who usually intermingle with the Mulan, are short, muscular and have dusky skin

FUN FACT
There are nine major ethnic human groups in the Forgotten Realms but even more smaller ones scattered around Faerûn!

Get ready to test your RPG fandom knowledge and see if you know the long-form version of these D&D acronyms.

1. AoE _____
2. HP _____
3. NPC _____
4. DM _____
5. RP _____
6. IC _____
7. PvP _____
8. RAW _____
9. SP _____
10. RAI _____
11. GP _____
12. OOC _____
13. DMPC _____
14. PvM _____
15. PvE _____
16. AC _____
17. ATK _____
18. PP _____
19. PH _____
20. TPK _____

Ring of...

Aside from weapons and armor, adventurers can also wear jewelry that bestows upon them certain attributes and enhancements. These are not your average silver and gold rings. The rings listed below are magical and grant the wearer extra perks. Each starts with the title "Ring of..." Can you unscramble them all?

1. ailnAm nfcInuele

   Hint: You can cast one of the following spells: animal friendship, fear, speak with animals

2. eFre Atncoi

   Hint: Difficult terrain doesn't cost any extra movement, and magic can't slow you down.

3. honSitgo stSar

   Hint: Allows you to cast dancing lights, light, faerie fire, and ball lightning.

4. eSlpl urnTgni

   Hint: Grants the wearer advantage on saving throws against spells targeting only them.

5. tThru elnTgli

   Hint: Allows the wearer to determine if someone is lying to them.

6. eaerthF nglFlia

   Hint: Allows the wearer to fall from great heights without taking any damage.

7. tsbiIniyilvi

   Hint: The wearer disappears from sight.

8. uzrPelsz tWi

   Hint: The wearer can use one charge to grant an advantage on an intelligence check.

9. dMin hinSilged

   Hint: Protects the user's brain from spells and deception.

10. onReeeanrtgi

    Hint: The wearer regains 1d6 hit points every ten minutes.

11. pSlle trSngoi

    Hint: This ring holds up to five levels of spells that the wearer can use if they are attuned to it.

FUN FACT

A character can only wear two rings at a time.

Diamond Maze

Make your way to the sparkling diamond at the end of the maze.

START

True Adventurer Trivia

Get ready to test your RPG fandom knowledge and answer as many trivia questions as you can about halflings.

1. How tall is a halfling?
   _____

2. How much does a halfling usually weigh?
   _____

3. What color hair does a halfling usually have?
   _____

4. Halflings don't have royalty among them; instead, they look to
   _____ to lead them.

5. Most halflings have what alignment?
   _____

6. Halflings have an advantage on saving throws against what?
   _____

7. What are the two subraces of halflings?
   _____

8. What ability score is increased for a lightfoot?
   _____

9. What ability score is increased for a stout?
   _____

10. What is a stout halfling resistant against?
    _____

11. What is a halfling's speed?
    _____

12. At what age does a halfling reach adulthood?
    _____

Skill Check Crossword

Each character has proficiency in different skills that aid (or sometimes hinder) them in their adventures through the multiverse. Being experienced in a specific skill can add dice roll bonuses to ability checks. Test your knowledge and see if you can identify the skills below using the clues given!

ACROSS

4. This skill encompasses activities that use physical strength like jumping, climbing and swimming
7. This skill shows how easily your character can stay on their feet and balance themselves
8. This allows players to aid ailing companions and allies
10. A player's ability to trick others and hide the truth
11. This skill handles your player's ability to put on a show using music, dancing, storytelling, and other forms of art
12. This allows players to detect lies and figure out a creature's true intentions
13. This skill looks at the player's knowledge of ancient deities, rituals, prayers, and symbols

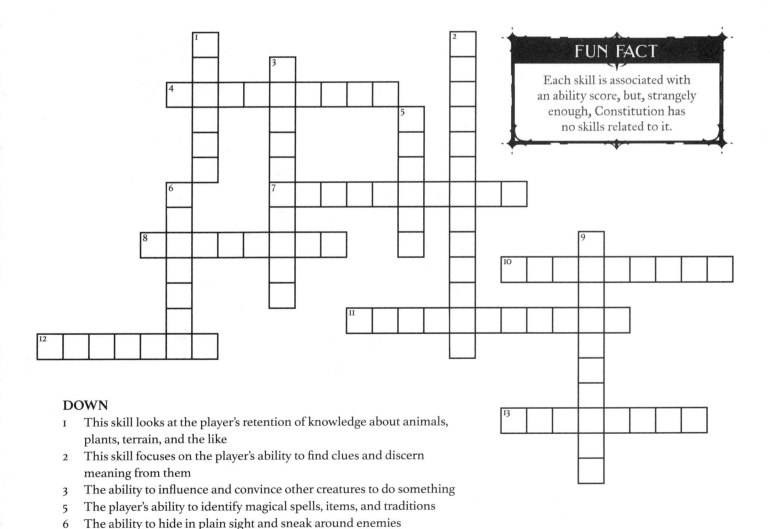

FUN FACT

Each skill is associated with an ability score, but, strangely enough, Constitution has no skills related to it.

DOWN

1. This skill looks at the player's retention of knowledge about animals, plants, terrain, and the like
2. This skill focuses on the player's ability to find clues and discern meaning from them
3. The ability to influence and convince other creatures to do something
5. The player's ability to identify magical spells, items, and traditions
6. The ability to hide in plain sight and sneak around enemies
9. This skill measures a player's awareness of their surroundings

Character Classes Word Search

One of the most important parts of creating your adventurer is to choose their class. Beyond simply being their job, it's their one true calling, and in some cases the reason they're adventuring to begin with. There are twelve distinct classes with different abilities to choose from in the 5th Edition of the *Dungeons & Dragons Player's Manual*. Can you find all the character classes in the word search below?

```
X C R Y D X Z A W D U S O V D B W H
W H S O A G K Z D R U I D H X D N A
U M W R G G P J A B J Y L J N N W O
H M P L X U J E S H P I C F X B X L
I B W C I G E M P L A Q L W W J D S
B Z A O A O B E O G L O E I M D M S
U X T R W U E X J N A D R Z S Q V Z
B Z W E B R B Q P Q D J I A X B E M
A Z X K G A I M S Z I P C R A X F O
F N R U D N R J G X N M O D E S K N
O G O A T H W I J H F J D B A R D K
E R Y O N B N Z A G L W A R L O C K
L S O L E G S P W N F R S Y A A Y V
B A V S N P E A V E V U A L G P J P
V B H S R U F R A U F I G H T E R O
W G M F K V R N F C F R B D D O Y N
S M K D V Q I S O R C E R E R J E K
T L M P N N B I Y M H J L J H H S E
```

barbarian	druid	paladin	sorcerer
bard	fighter	ranger	warlock
cleric	monk	rogue	wizard

FUN FACT

The fighter is the most played character class in Dungeons & Dragons!

Wondrous Items

On your adventures you may stumble upon various items in each dungeon, ruin, or even village you step foot into. Some of these items are magical and possess qualities that set them apart from ordinary adventuring items. These fantastical things are called wondrous items and there are quite a few lying about Faerûn. Using the clues, unscramble each word to find out the name of some wondrous items you can find on your adventures.

1. scdAabbarru

   _____

   Hint: A wooden chest with gemstones that weighs 25 pounds when empty.

2. rceAan mirroGie

   _____

   Hint: A leather-bound book that can be used to gain a bonus on spell attack rolls and saving throws.

3. gBa of nlogdHi

   _____

   Hint: Where players can store all of their items.

4. aBeancl of nraymHo

   _____

   Hint: A scale that you can use to cast the ritual "detect evil and good."

5. koBo fo eVli arsDensk

   _____

   Hint: A manuscript filled with horrors no mortal should see. It can cause the reader to go mad.

6. Cneald of hte eDep

   _____

   Hint: This item's flame cannot be extinguished when placed in water.

7. oHok fo issFehr elhDtig

   _____

   Hint: This item, when attached to a fishing line and tossed in water, can conjure a fish.

8. odeLntaos

   _____

   Hint: Cursed gem worth 150 gp. It reduces the player's speed by 5 and halves their load and lift capacities.

9. Nitgh lraCel

   _____

   Hint: You can cast the "animate dead spell" if this whistle is blown in the darkness.

10. brO fo iTme

    _____

    Hint: When used, this gives the ability to determine if it's night, day, evening, or afternoon outside.

11. pPare riDb

    _____

    Hint: The user writes a message on this paper and whispers the name of a recipient that it will fly to.

Fun Fact

Wondrous items are magical items that don't fit into other categories like armor or weapons.

Dungeon Maze

Make your way through the dungeon maze to reach the gem at the center.

START

Well-Known Characters Crossword

DUNGEONS & DRAGONS spans many multimedia productions, including books, movies, and video games. Each of these iterations feature their own prominent characters that undergo various trials and tribulations through the multiverse. Whether they're treasure hunters, dragon slayers, fierce kings, or even gods themselves, the D&D universe is full of rich characters with exciting backgrounds. The characters in the puzzle below are some of the most beloved and well known among both fans and critics alike. Can you identify them all?

ACROSS

1. Former wizard and lich king, this powerful villain became the God of Secrets
3. Creator of the legendary warhammer called Aegis-fang that was bestowed upon Wulgar
5. Created by R. A. Salavatore, this drow has gone against the evil ways of his people in the Underdark
7. Both a protagonist and antagonist of the *Dragonlance* novels, this skilled wizard is after the power of ancient wizards
9. A cleric and follower of Shar that appears in *Baldur's Gate 3*
10. An ancient vampire who rules over Barovia

DOWN

2. A white-haired vampire from the popular video game *Baldur's Gate 3*
4. An old mage in the Forgotten Realms who is considered a Chosen of Mystra
6. A ranger from Baldur's Gate that is often found talking to a hamster named Boo
8. A half elf druid that shows up in the *Baldur's Gate* game series

FUN FACT

As of 2024, there are 299 published DUNGEONS & DRAGONS books that take place in the Forgotten Realms. This includes novels, anthology, and novellas.

True Adventurer Trivia

Get ready to test your RPG fandom knowledge and answer as many trivia questions as you can. Answer these true or false questions to the best of your ability.

1. Druidic allows players to leave hidden messages.

   _____

2. Elves need more sleep than their human counterparts.

   _____

3. Humans only have one god.

   _____

4. Druids can take on the form of an animal.

   _____

5. Standard coins weigh about one-third of an ounce.

   _____

6. You can break up player movement with an action.

   _____

7. It is generally hard to gain a dwarf's trust.

   _____

8. Tieflings mature at the same rate as humans.

   _____

DEITIES CROSSWORD

Religion plays an important part in the lives of many adventurers throughout the multiverse. While some characters don't believe in any gods, there are devout worshippers who follow the teachings of a single deity or pantheon of gods. Doing so offers characters, like acolytes, bonuses to their skill proficiencies and gives them a life purpose in a vast world of opportunities. It's up to your Dungeon Master to choose which deities can be worshipped in their campaign. Using the clues at the bottom of the puzzle, identify the deities worshipped throughout Faerûn.

ACROSS
2. God of knowledge
7. Goddess of magic
10. God of writing
11. Goddess of darkness and loss
12. Goddess of love and beauty

FUN FACT
Pelor is one of the most worshipped deities by humans. He is the god of various things including agriculture, sun, strength, light, and healing.

DOWN
1. God of protection
3. God of wizards
4. Goddess of the sea
5. God of storms
6. God of craft
8. God of tyranny
9. God of lies

Heart of Eternity Diamond Maze

Make your way to the sparkling Heart of Eternity diamond at the end of the maze.

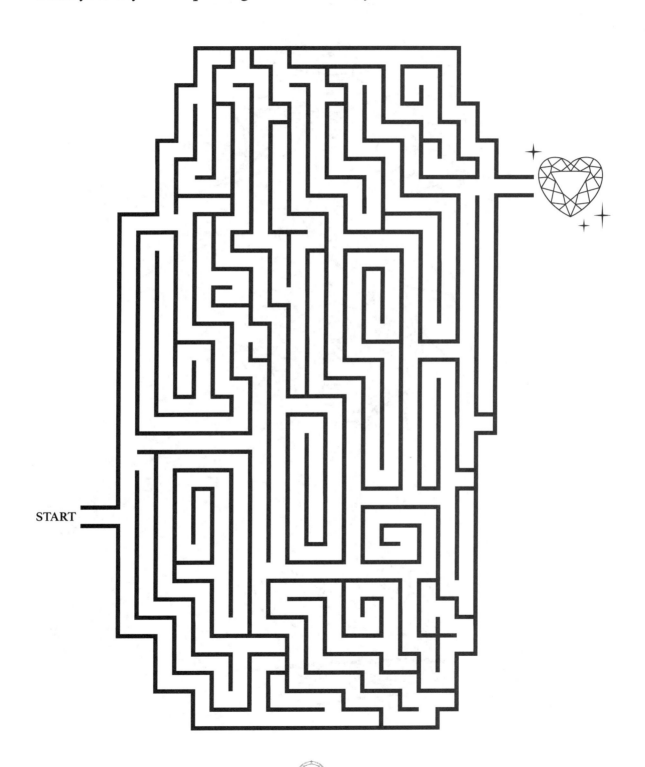

Weapon of Choice Word Search

Character class, feats, and race give players proficiency in a weapon. There are many to choose from, ranging from simple weapons like a small knife to more intricate ones like the war pick. Martial weapons need a bit more skilled training to wield properly but are generally more effective. Which weapons will your adventurer find in this puzzle?

```
C R O S S B O W X J H B S N G J J Z
H Q M N W N H S Q R T D O S E R O G
D L H U C I U T Q C E Y S R L T P Y
A A A K L J N T E Z Q Y H A C I R A
G K S H U A G R E A T C L U B N N F
G O H W B V Q L E L S G P M A X J G
E Y O O Z E Z B H A N D A X E T C J
R G R Q B L O W G U N L Y Q Y D H E
W J T P F I J T S G C V S I Z W A H
X F B I L N Z G E E Q V M B K E M M
K Q O S A M L A M J Y M A C E S M U
A E W T Q U A R T E R S T A F F E S
K R R O O Y P D Y P P P B N F M C R K
S N V L F X M W V R J K E Y R B W E
N O S P E A R S I C K L E T D A R T
N K E V Q C M O P S L A E Y H J Z G
O R O E U R R N A Q Y H S X B R P B
L O N G B O W F F O N H C M K G K G
```

blowgun	dart	javelin	net	sickle
club	greatclub	longbow	pistol	sling
crossbow	hammer	mace	quarterstaff	spear
dagger	handaxe	musket	shortbow	

FUN FACT

Adventurers can use improvised weapons if they have no other ones equipped. These usually deal 1d4 damage.

Castle Quest Maze

Make your way through the castle to the end of the maze.

True Adventurer Trivia

Get ready to test your RPG fandom knowledge and answer as many trivia questions as you can. Give it a go and see what sections of the player manual you're proficient in.

1. How many languages should your character speak?
   _____

2. What is the highest level your character can reach?
   _____

3. What is a tiny trinket?
   _____

4. What type of armor is chain mail?
   _____

5. How many categories of armor are there?
   _____

6. What happens if a player or creature is three-quarters in cover?
   _____

7. Unless otherwise specified, creatures usually have a _____ foot reach when attacking.

8. You can only control a mount for the player to ride under these conditions:
   _____

9. What is the lowest a player's or a creature's hit points can reach?
   _____

10. What happens when you score a critical hit?
    _____

11. What are the four main ways players can restore their hit points?
    _____

Dungeon Maze

Find your way through the dungeon rooms to complete your quest.

Halfling Names Word Search

Halflings live in small peaceful villages with large farms and groves. They prefer to keep to their own traditions no matter how many years go by. Similar to gnomes, halflings can often find themselves with several names. They can have their personal given name, a family name, and a nickname. Below are several different halfling names. Can you find them all?

```
T P A E L A S W X W A K A Z E Q X N
K T E A L E A F O C N C B P T W K N
L I V L P D E U P H E M I A M Z Q G
L J T N C X G B R U S H G A T H E R
H F V H I P O H D Q O M Y S K U P I
G Y S J R S O J X W N S C J L N R M
F C I L H I D A A A T Z Q Q N D H D
C M G L I U B G X E D A J H J E T R
Z P R G G D A T Q F Z O B I L R O C
B W E T H O R N G A G E R L E B S V
S I E C H A R F Z I Z A R L A O S B
M G N T I V E I E L D O N T G U C L
E B B Q L G L N A U I M E O A G O W
R P O E L J Z N L G X U D P L H B P
R G T J O P L A R H T K D P L E B P
I H T R D S A N X T N R A L O V L F
C E L Z P C A H N W J Y E E W C E W
R R E O S B O R N F F I F W Q Y K D
```

brushgather	goodbarrel	kithri	osborn	tosscobble
eldon	greenbottle	leagallow	paela	underbough
euphemia	highhill	merric	tealeaf	
finnan	hilltopple	nedda	thorngage	

FUN FACT

A family name for a halfling usually always started as a nickname that stuck for generations!

True Adventurer Trivia

Get ready to test your RPG fandom knowledge and answer as many trivia questions as you can about gnomes.

1. How tall is a gnome on average?
   _____

2. How much does a gnome weigh on average?
   _____

3. What prominent features does a gnome usually have?
   _____

4. **TRUE OR FALSE:** Gnomes are natural jokesters.
   _____

5. Gnomes who live in human lands often have what professions?
   _____

6. What is the average lifespan of a gnome?
   _____

7. What ability score increases for a gnome?
   _____

8. What alignment does a gnome have?
   _____

9. At what age do gnomes mature into adulthood?
   _____

10. What are the subraces of gnomes?
    _____

11. What cantrips do forest gnomes start with?
    _____

12. Rock gnomes are proficient with which tools?
    _____

Magical Weapons

There is a plethora of weapons all around the multiverse. You may sometimes come upon a sparkling weapon that doesn't look like your usual longsword or staff. These weapons are usually enchanted and magical in nature. Here are just a few magical weapons that you can find in various Dungeons & Dragons campaigns. Use the clues to help you unscramble the words and identify each weapon.

1. allBufe Tanlo

   _____

   Hint: An obsidian dagger that grants a +1 to attack and damage rolls.

2. zueAgerd

   _____

   Hint: A sentient battleaxe forged by the wizard Ahghairon to defend Waterdeep.

3. oetBnornecu

   _____

   Hint: A magical mace that grants the user +1 silver piece every time an undead is slain.

4. Frtos rnBad

   _____

   Hint: A magic sword that grants 1d6 cold damage and shines a bright light in freezing temperatures.

5. necLtu seDtyrreo

   _____

   Hint: A triple barrel musket that allows you to cast dancing lights if attuned to it.

6. oMon eikcSl

   _____

   Hint: Bathed in moonlight, this silver-bladed sickle grants the wielder a bonus to spell attack rolls and saving throw DCs of the player's druid and ranger spells.

7. aksRdo eeniikRtf

   _____

   Hint: A legendary dagger that imprisons the soul of a creature that is slain using it. The dagger can hold up to five souls.

8. tartseeiphSk

   _____

   Hint: An uncommon longsword that grants +1 bonus to attack and damage rolls. If it strikes an object, the hit is critical.

9. kesdriteTrni

   _____

   Hint: A legendary flint dagger that emanates sparks from its edges when it hits a solid object.

10. Vrloap wrSod

    _____

    Hint: Gain a +3 bonus to attack and damage rolls with this magic weapon. The blade also ignores any resistances to slashing damage.

11. htyWea

    _____

    Hint: A legendary sentient greatsword with a neutral good alignment. A giant takes extra 2d6 slashing from this weapon and will fall prone if a DC 15 strength saving throw is not rolled.

FUN FACT

Any weapon type can be magical, including staffs and bows.

Get ready to test your RPG fandom knowledge and answer as many trivia questions as you can.

1. When a monster reaches zero hit points, does it die or drop unconscious?
   _____

2. What are the three pillars of D&D play?
   _____

3. Which of these is not an official D&D setting?
   A) Dark Sun
   B) Ravenloft
   C) Moonsly
   D) Dragonlance

4. What do you call a full-length D&D adventure?
   _____

5. What are four movement types that players can use?
   _____

6. What spell can revive a fallen (deceased) character?
   _____

7. When you have zero health points, how many successful death-saving throws do you need to become stable?
   _____

8. How many copper pieces are worth one gold piece?
   _____

D&D Bingo

During your next campaign, try out this bingo card and see how many events you and your party complete.

HOW TO PLAY:

Mark an X in the middle of the board. This is your free space. Every time you or a member of your party completes an activity on the board, draw an X on that space. Five spaces marked in a row means bingo—you win!

NAT 20	MET A BARD ON YOUR TRAVELS	SLAYED A DRAGON	PARTY MEMBER DIED	SUCCESSFULLY PICKPOCKETED SOMEONE
FAILED A PERCEPTION CHECK	FOUND A RARE ARTIFACT	DEFEATED TWO ENEMIES WITH ONE HIT	ACCIDENTALLY STOLE SOMETHING	ROLL THE SAME NUMBER TWICE
DIDN'T HIT A SINGLE ENEMY IN COMBAT	BROKE CHARACTER		NAT 1	COMPLETED A QUEST FOR AN NPC
LONG REST	SESSION ENDED EARLY	TALKED TO AN ANIMAL	HAD A BIG MEAL AT CAMP	BARD SANG A SONG
A CHARACTER LEVELED UP	HAD TO SPEAK IN ANOTHER LANGUAGE BESIDES COMMON	SHORT REST	REVIVED A PARTY MEMBER	SPOKE TO THE DEAD

ANSWERS:

PAGE 4

1. Polyhedral
2. False
3. Strength, Dexterity, Wisdom, Constitution, Intelligence, Charisma
4. Candles will brighten a 5-foot radius and provide a dimmer light for another five feet.
5. Navigator's tools allow players to chart a course on sea, but they must be proficient in the skill.
6. Intelligence
7. On the Upper Planes
8. Stat Blocks
9. Those that have no form or are Huge or Gargantuan.

PAGE 6

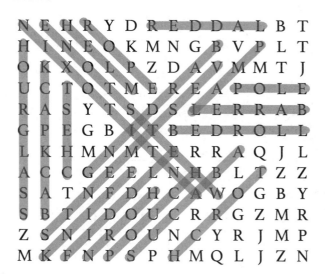

PAGE 7

1. Death Ward
2. Guidance
3. Bless
4. Flame Strike
5. Earthquake
6. Divination
7. Holy Aura
8. True Seeing
9. Astral Projection
10. Revivify
11. Raise Dead
12. Blade Barrier
13. Heroes Feast
14. Commune
15. Heal

PAGE 8

```
N E H R Y D R E D D A L B T
H I N E O K M N G B V P L T
O K X O L P Z D A V M M T J
U C T O T M E R E A P O L E
R A S Y T S D S L E R R A B
G P E G B I T B E D R O L L
L K H M N M T E R R A Q J L
A C C G E E L N H B L T Z Z
S A T N F D H C A W O G B Y
S B T I D O U C R R G Z M R
Z S N I R O U N C Y R J M P
M K F N P S P H M Q L J Z N
```

PAGE 9

May the dice be ever be in your favor

PAGE 10

```
X I B D T G B F V O Z V Y S F L T B
R G L S V T V X D O F L G M G C N E
J B E L E P H A N T M O J S E Y D U
X O A I N T B R E V D N P O X L D S
E O E I S B N H P O V G U O W T G H
Y Y Z I R X S S F I M S N Q N G T L
F P L G S Q V B M U H T U W Y G V
H W A A M Y H K T A L I K N A L K V
R A L L H Q W I N S E P P F R Z W D
V D I L S D Q E P T O P W H H C A Q
I H W E A M V W M I O J Y F O E R Y
T O K Y T M H K J F Y W P D R K S C
V R R O W B O A T F B M Q L S D H A
G S H N M H A B H Z F N U R E R I M
U E P J V K P P K E E L B O A T P E
D R G U F S I E U A K U S C H U B L
C S P A O Z L Y V Y G H N P D G N R
H O L N L J Y I G V D B E Z L X K B
```

86

PAGE 12

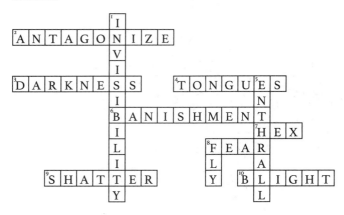

PAGE 14

PAGE 15

1. Player's Handbook
2. Monster Manual
3. Dungeon Master's Guide
4. Eve of Ruin
5. The Druid's Call
6. Honor Among Thieves
7. Mindbreaker
8. Warriors and Weapons
9. Tomb of Annihilation
10. Curse of Strahd

PAGE 17

1. By rolling a d20.
2. Players can use heroic inspiration to roll the dice again and use that new number in place of the old one.
3. False
4. One hour
5. 6 seconds
6. The order of turns
7. False
8. 9

PAGE 18

1. Potion of Aqueous Form
2. Oil of Etherealness
3. Mummy of Rot Antidote
4. Elixir of Health
5. Potion of Flying
6. Philter of Love
7. Oil of Sharpness
8. Potion of Vitality
9. Blood of the Lycanthrope Antidote
10. Bottled Breath
11. Potion of Watchful Rest
12. Thessaltoxin Antidote

PAGE 19

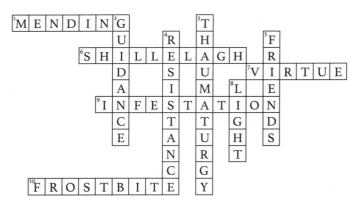

87

PAGE 20

START

PAGE 22

PAGE 24

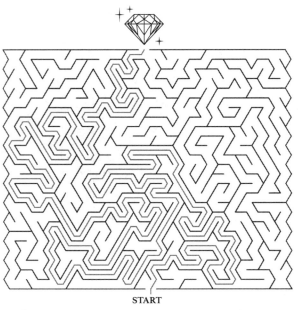

START

PAGE 25

1. Bahamut and Tiamat
2. No
3. Bronze to Brass
4. Taller (usually well over 6 feet)
5. More (about 200-300 pounds)
6. three fingers and a thumb
7. Uncommon
8. Strength and Charisma
9. 15
10. 30 feet
11. Medium
12. 10

PAGE 26

Acid–25GP

Antitoxin–50GP

Book–25GP

Fine Clothes–15GP

Tent–2GP

Magnifying Glass–100GP

Backpack–2GP

Bedroll–1GP

Basic Poison–100GP

Scholar's Pack–40GP

Lock–10GP

Shovel–2GP

PAGE 27

PAGE 28

1. Clothes of Mending
2. Boots of the Winterlands
3. Blasted Goggles
4. Amulet of the Devout
5. Cloak of Displacement
6. Circlet of Human Perfection
7. Clockwork Amulet
8. Dread Helm
9. Crown of Lies
10. Gauntlets of Ogre Power
11. Hat of Disguise
12. Jester's Mask
13. Bracers of Celerity

PAGE 29

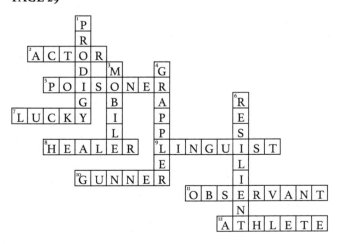

PAGE 31

PAGE 32

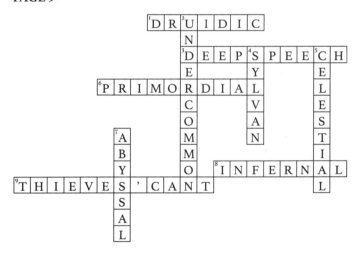

PAGE 33

1. Constitution
2. Lawful
3. Resistance against poison
4. Battleaxe, handaxe, throwing hammer, and warhammer
5. Hill dwarves and mountain dwarves
6. Wisdom +1
7. hill dwarf
8. +2 strength
9. 350 years

PAGE 35

1. 16
2. Magic Initiate
3. Acrobatics and Performance
4. Herbalism kit
5. Strength, Dexterity, Constitution
6. Three
7. Gives allies who listen to it, heroic inspiration
8. Skilled
9. Athlete
10. Two per short or long rest. (At 20th level, the Archdruid feature grants unlimited uses.)
11. Two
12. Six

PAGE 36

PAGE 37

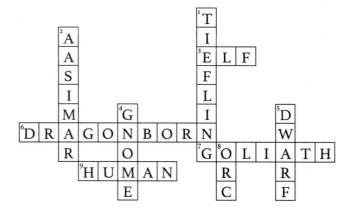

PAGE 39

START

PAGE 40

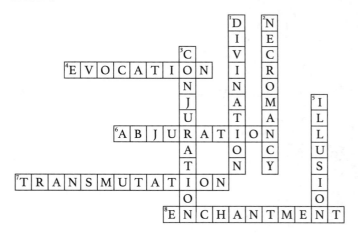

PAGE 42

1. The Rise of Tiamat
2. Lost Mine of Phandelver
3. Out of the Abyss
4. Candlekeep Mysteries
5. Ghosts of Saltmarsh
6. Tomb of Annihilation
7. Waterdeep Dragon Heist
8. Storm King's Thunder
9. Hoard of the Dragon Queen

PAGE 44

1. Stranger Things
2. Mazes and Monsters
3. E.T.
4. four
5. The Book of Vile Darkness
6. b ($208 million)
7. c (2000)
8. a (1983)
9. three

PAGE 45

PAGE 46

PAGE 47

1. 100-145 pounds
2. True
3. Small forest villages
4. Corellon
5. 750 years
6. Dark Elf/Drow, High Elves, Wood Elves
7. Dexterity +2
8. Evil
9. 30 feet
10. They have Perception skill because of Keen Senses
11. High elf

PAGE 49

PAGE 51

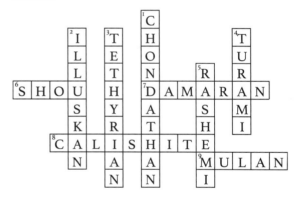

PAGE 52

(crossword)

PAGE 53

1. Area of Effect
2. Health Points
3. Non-Playable Characters
4. Dungeon Master
5. Roleplay
6. In-Character
7. Player versus Player
8. Rules as Written
9. Silver Pieces
10. Rules as Intended
11. Gold Pieces
12. Out Of Character
13. Dungeon Master's Player Character
14. Player versus Monster
15. Player versus Environment
16. Armor Class
17. Attack
18. Passive Perception
19. Player's Handbook
20. Total Party Kill

PAGE 55

1. Animal Influence
2. Free Action
3. Shooting Stars
4. Spell Turning
5. Truth Telling
6. Feather Falling
7. Invisibility
8. Puzzler's Wit
9. Mind Shielding
10. Regeneration
11. Spell Storing

PAGE 57

PAGE 58

1. 3ft
2. 40-45 pounds
3. Brown
4. Family elders
5. Lawful good
6. Being Frightened
7. Stout, Lightfoot
8. Charisma
9. Constitution
10. Poison
11. 25 feet
12. 20

PAGE 59

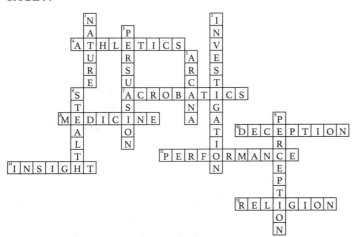

PAGE 63

PAGE 61

PAGE 62

1. Abracadbrus
2. Arcane Grimoire
3. Bag of Holding
4. Balance of Harmony
5. Book of Vile Darkness
6. Candle of the Deep
7. Hook of Fisher's Delight
8. Loadstone
9. Night Caller
10. Orb of Time
11. Paper Bird

PAGE 64

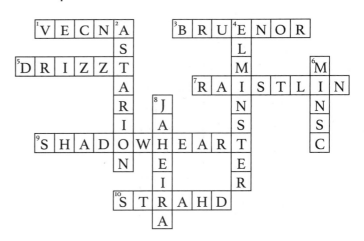

PAGE 66

1. True
2. False
3. False
4. True
5. True
6. True
7. True
8. True

PAGE 68

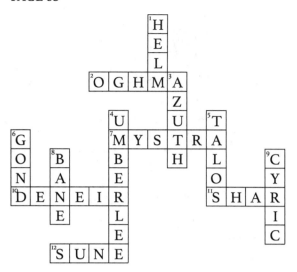

PAGE 69

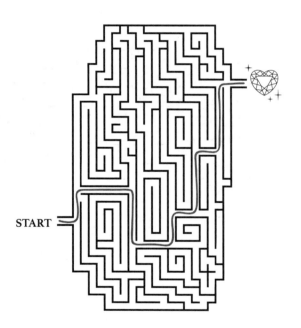

PAGE 71

PAGE 73

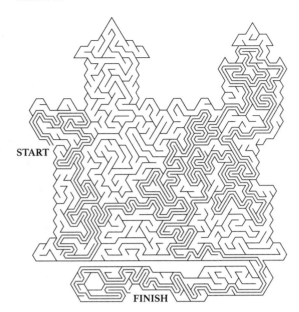

PAGE 75

1. Three
2. Level 20
3. A small object that has been touched by mystery that players can get when they make their character
4. Heavy
5. Three
6. There is a +5 bonus added to their AC and Dexterity saving throws.
7. 5 foot
8. If the creature is trained to hold a rider.
9. Zero
10. Players will be able to roll the attack damage twice and add the total together, plus any additional modifiers.
11. Short rest, long rest, healing spell, or a healing potion.

PAGE 77

PAGE 79

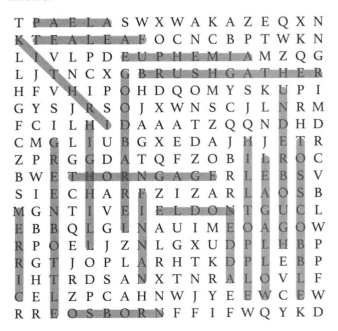

PAGE 81

1. 3 feet
2. 40-45 pounds
3. Brown or tan skin, fair hair and small build
4. True
5. Gemcutters, engineers, sages, tinkers
6. 350-500 years
7. Intelligence
8. Good
9. 40
10. Forest gnome, rock gnome
11. Minor Illusion
12. Artisan's or Tinker Tools

PAGE 83

1. Baleful Talon
2. Azuredge
3. Bonecounter
4. Frost Brand
5. Lucent Destroyer
6. Moon Sickle
7. Rakdos Riteknife
8. Shatterspike
9. Tinderstrike
10. Vorpal Sword
11. Waythe

PAGE 84

1. It dies.
2. Social interaction, exploration, combat
3. Moonsly
4. Campaign
5. climbing, crawling, jumping, swimming
6. Raise Dead
7. Three
8. 100